Mr. Wolf moved into the empty house beside the chicken coop. "Right next door to dinner," he chuckled, rubbing his paws together.

He put on his speckled tie, his feather-patterned vest, his egg brooch and his chicken watch. Then he went to introduce himself to the hens.

"How do you do?" he said sweetly, leaning over the fence. "How are you today?"

"We're fine," said the chickens. "Just clucky. Thank you very much!" And they all giggled, the way chickens do.

"Would you care to join me for dinner?" said Mr. Wolf. "This evening?"

"WHAT TIME IS IT, MR. WOLF?"

8 O'CLUCK

JILL CREIGHTON

PIERRE-PAUL PARISEAU

SCHOLASTIC INC.
New York Toronto London Auckland Sydney

To Sam, Eric and Will,
with love.
— J.C

To Eve, my love.
— P.-P.P

The cut-and-paste illustration technique used in this book is called photomontage. Images were collected from magazines, brochures, catalogues — anything lying around the house.

ISBN 0-590-93568-2

Text copyright © 1995 by Jill Creighton.
Illustrations copyright © 1995 by Pierre-Paul Pariseau.
All rights reserved. Published by Scholastic Inc., by arrangement with Scholastic Canada Ltd.

12 11 10 9 8 7 6 5 4 3 2   7 8 9/9 0 1 2/0
                                                                  09

Printed in the U.S.A.

First Scholastic printing, March 1997

"How kind," said the chickens.
Mr. Wolf grinned. "I'll pick you up at eight," he said.
The chickens looked at his beautiful watch.
"What time is it, Mr. Wolf?"
"One o'cluck," said Mr. Wolf. He smiled craftily to himself,
thinking what a very big stew he would be able to make.

ONE O'CLUCK

3

Mr. Wolf went home and cleaned his kitchen to get ready for his chicken dinner.

"Those chickens will never guess my plan," he snickered. "They're such pea-brains."

He washed dishes and dried dishes, he swept the floor and wiped the counters. His chores took him one hour.

The chickens passed by his window carrying coils of rope.

"What time is it, Mr. Wolf?" they called.

Mr. Wolf stuck his head out the window.

"Two o'cluck." He smiled politely, showing his long white teeth, and wondered about the rope.

5

Mr. Wolf pulled his head back in and opened the kitchen cupboard to drag out his largest pot. It was dirty and a spider had laid eggs in it.

He scrubbed and cleaned and polished the pot till it glowed, then rolled it over to the fireplace and lifted it onto an iron hook. That took him one hour.

The chickens passed by his window wheeling wooden boards in a wheelbarrow.

"What time is it, Mr. Wolf?" they giggled.

"Three o'cluck," he answered. "Those chickens certainly are busy," he murmured, absent-mindedly rubbing his belly.

THREE O' CLUC

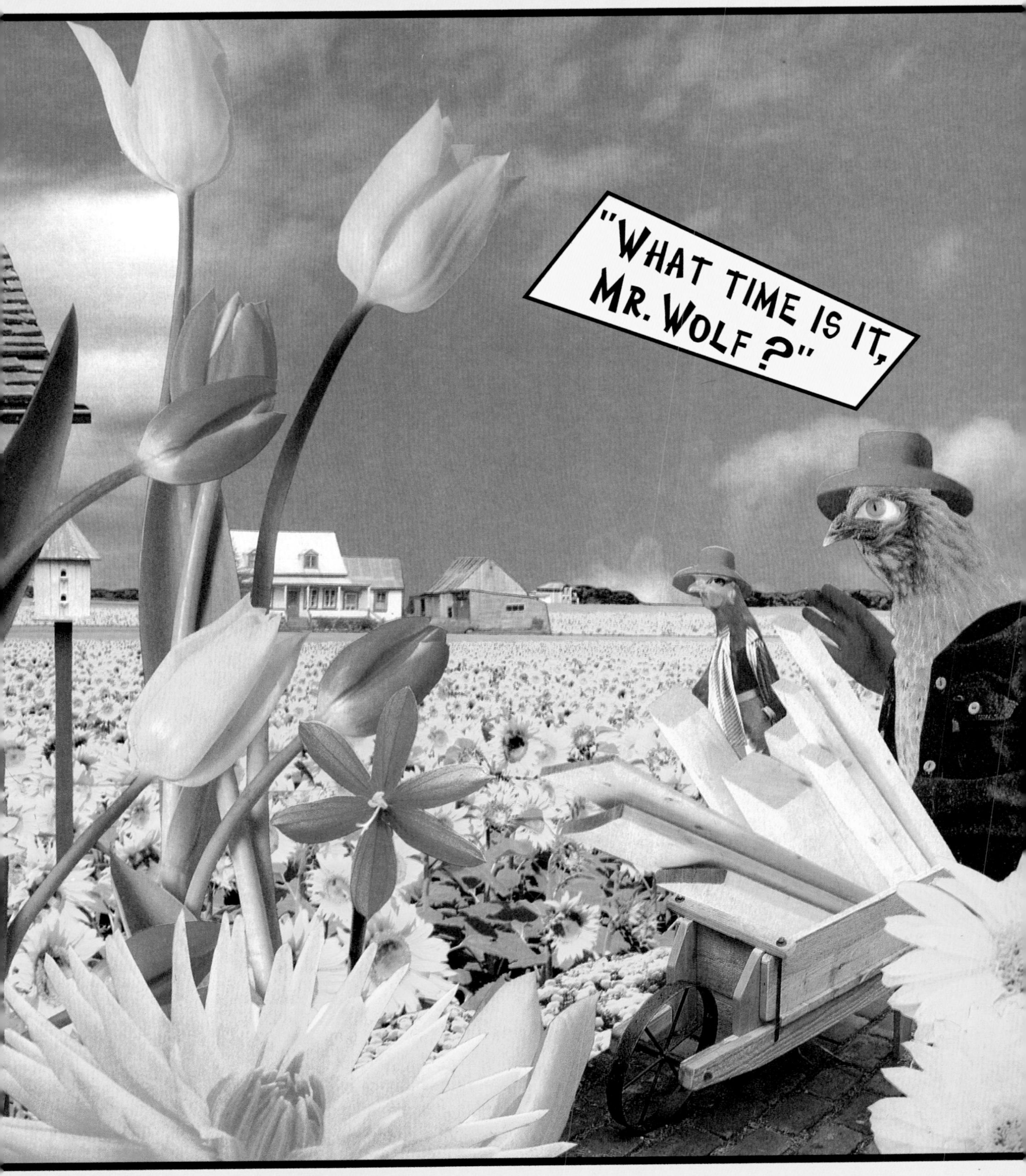
"WHAT TIME IS IT,
MR. WOLF ?"

FOUR O'CLUCK

Mr. Wolf began carrying buckets of water from the stream to fill up the big pot. He made fourteen trips, back and forth. All that carrying took him one hour.

On his last trip up from the stream, Mr. Wolf met the chickens carrying bags of nails, hammers and two big padlocks.

"What time is it, Mr. Wolf?" they asked.

"Four o'cluck," he answered, licking his lips. "I've never seen such busy chickens," he thought. The chickens winked and smiled and waved as they passed by.

Mr. Wolf went out into the forest with a sack to gather wood for his fire. He dragged it home and laid the dry sticks neatly under the pot, all ready to light. Gathering the wood took him one hour.

There was a lot of noise — hammering, banging, squawking — coming from next door. Mr. Wolf went out and peeked over the fence to see what was going on. The chickens were building a big crate.

"Chickens building!" Mr. Wolf chuckled to himself. "How ridiculous!"

Three chickens stood in the yard near the fence. "What time is it, Mr. Wolf?" they asked, smiling sweetly.

"Five o'cluck," he answered, drooling down his furry chin.

FIVE O'

Mr. Wolf hurried home and cut up a big stack of vegetables to go in the chicken stew: carrots, onions, celery, potatoes and some green pepper.

"Dumplings would go nicely," he said to himself, and he mixed up a batch of thick batter and set the bowl aside with a cloth over it. The chopping and mixing took him one hour.

Then Mr. Wolf peeked out his door. The chickens were all inside the henhouse, gathered around the telephone. One chicken poked her head out.

SIX O'CLUCK

"What time is it, Mr. Wolf?" she called.
"Six o'cluck," he answered, staring at her fat belly.
She slammed the door.
"Rude," he murmured, "but pleasingly plump!"

15

Mr. Wolf decided to set the table. First he ironed his best tablecloth and smoothed it over the table. He laid out his shiniest silver, his chicken platter, and a bright red napkin to go around his neck. In the center of the table he placed a large silver dish to catch the bones, and a glass full of peppermint-flavored toothpicks.

On the kitchen counter he set his sharp knives, his ladles, his spoons and a chopping board, all in a row. All this took him one hour.

The chickens were pecking in the yard, but they lifted their heads and fluttered their wingtips at Mr. Wolf when he came out.

"What time is it, Mr. Wolf?" they cackled.

"Seven o'cluck," he murmured in a quiet, crafty voice. Soon it would be dark.

Mr. Wolf went indoors humming to himself. He covered the pot and lit the fire to heat the water.

Next door he heard a truck backing up, so he peeked out the window. The chickens were struggling to lift the big crate they had built into the truck. Three pigs were helping them.

"Eggs going out," Mr. Wolf thought, and flicked the curtains shut. He went to hunt for some clean cloth sacks, and a pillowcase to save the feathers.

Then Mr. Wolf took
off his speckled tie, his
feather-patterned vest
and his egg brooch, and
he laid his chicken
watch gently on top of
the dresser. One hour
had crept by.

His stomach was rumbling as he tiptoed down the front steps. His claws were itching as he sneaked toward the chicken coop and slithered through the gate. His teeth were glistening as he pushed open the door of the henhouse with his chilly black nose.

The chickens cackled in front of their mirrors and fluffed up their feathers. Each of them turned one bright eye toward the door. "What time is it, Mr. Wolf?" they lisped daintily.

DINNER TIME!

"DINNER TIME!" roared Mr. Wolf, and he leaped inside. There was a screeching and a growling, a thumping and bumping, a scuffling and a yowling and a squawking.

The henhouse door burst open. Out came Mr. Wolf, followed by all the chickens. He bounced down the path, trussed up tighter than a holiday turkey, tied in a hundred knots. His toes stuck out one end, his nose out the other,

and his tail flopped along like an old feather duster.

The chickens twirled him over to the truck. The three pigs rolled him up the ramp. Everyone jostled him into the crate, slammed it shut, and snapped on the two big padlocks.

Before Mr. Wolf knew what had happened, the pigs jumped into the truck, started up the engine, and roared away down the road.

The chickens fell to the ground, giggling hilariously. At last, with tears running down their beaks, they got up and went next door.

All laid out for them was a lovely feast: chopped carrots, onions, celery, potatoes and some green pepper. There was even batter for dumplings!